Anthony Best

by Davene Fahy

Illustrated by Carol Inouye

Sky Pony Press
New York

Sky Pony Press books may be purchased in bulk at special discounts for sales promotion, corporate gifts, fund-raising, or educational purposes. Special editions can also be created to specifications. For details, contact the Special Sales Department, Sky Pony Press, 307 West 36th Street, 11th Floor, New York, NY 10018 or info@skyhorsepublishing.com.

Sky Pony® is a registered trademark of Skyhorse Publishing, Inc.®, a Delaware corporation.

Visit our website at www.skyponypress.com.

10 9 8 7 6 5 4 3 2 1

Manufactured in China, September 2012
This product conforms to CPSIA 2008

Library of Congress Cataloging-in-Publication Data is available on file.

ISBN: 978-1-61608-961-0

For all the Anthonys I have known.

My next door friend is Anthony.

If you ask Anthony his name, he always says,

"My name is Anthony Best and I am the best boy."

But do you want to know a secret?

He's not always the best boy.

Sometimes he screams.

But that's usually when noises are really loud.

Anthony hates loud sounds.

6

Or when someone calls him "Tony."
Anthony doesn't like changes
and that means you better always call him
"Anthony" or be ready to hear a scream.

Anthony understands me,

but he doesn't look at me when I talk to him.

But I get him to look at me 'cause I look right

at him and I say,

"Hey Anthony, look at me!"

And he does, sometimes!

And sometimes Anthony will do weird things like one time he started to cross our street without even looking for cars.

But that's 'cause Anthony doesn't understand that it's dangerous.
Well it's good that not many cars come down our street so his Mom can always get him.

13

Anthony likes to play by himself,

but I like to play with Anthony.

Sometimes when he's in a spinning mood,
I'll spin too.

And when he's in a flipping mood,

I'll flip my pages too.

That makes Anthony happy.
And I know he's happy when he flaps
his hands.

Once when Tommy and I were playing
in the sand box,
Anthony threw sand at me and Tommy said
that was bad and he wasn't going to play
with Anthony any more.

But I said that was Anthony's way of playing with us.

And I showed Anthony how I put sand in a bucket.

19

The other day Tommy came over and said,

"Did you hear this knock knock joke?"

"Knock, Knock."

"Who's there?" I said.

"Boo."

"Boo who?" I said.

And Tommy said, "Don't cry. It's only a joke."

And we both laughed and laughed.

But Anthony didn't laugh. He didn't see

what was funny.

He just said, "I'm a friendly honey bee and

I'm going to be your friendly."

Last week this big, huge truck came
to Anthony's house.
And guess what was in it? A piano.

I didn't think those mover guys were ever
going to get that piano into Anthony's house.
But they did, after they took the door off.

23

The next day I heard this great music coming

from Anthony's house.

I knocked on the door and Mrs. Best answered.

I didn't understand what was going on.

I said, "I heard this beautiful music.

I thought you were playing the piano."

Mrs. Best said, "Come in, Hannah."

And there was Anthony, sitting at that big, black piano and playing a song I never heard before.

Wow! I can't do that and Tommy can't either.

So you know, when it comes to music,
Anthony really is the best boy.

Autism spectrum disorder (a neurobiological disorder) includes Autism Disorder, Pervasive Developmental Delay and Asperger's Syndrome. The precise relationships among these disorders is still being sorted out.

According to the National Institutes of Health, individuals with autism can be characterized primarily by developmental difficulties in verbal and non-verbal communication, social relating and leisure and play activities. People with these spectrum disorders often exhibit unusual repetitive movements and resistance to change in routines.

Higher functioning children (often labeled Asperger's Syndrome) may have language but have poor social skills, language problems and difficulty with play. They often have supersensitivity to sound and touch, temper tantrums and other erratic behaviors. They may have fixations and obsessive behavior. They occasionally have extraordinary skills not exhibited by most children.

These disorders typically last throughout a person's lifetime though symptoms range from very mild to quite severe. Although there is no cure, with early intervention, these symptoms can be modified.

For more information about autism spectrum disorders you might want to check the following websites:
> http://www.autism-society.org
> http://www.cureautismnow.com
> http://www.autism-resources.com
> http://www.nimh.nih.gov/publicat/autism.cfm

DAVENE FAHY, MA, CCC/SLP has worked as a Speech Therapist and Special Education Director for more than 40 years in the Philadelphia area and in Maine. She is a Life Member of the American Speech and Hearing Association (ASHA). She is the author of CHARLIE WHO COULDN'T SAY HIS NAME and THE BOY WHO THOUGHT HE WAS A PLANE. She lives on the coast of Maine with her husband, the writer Christopher Fahy.

CAROL INOUYE has written and/or illustrated more than a dozen children's books. She has also done illustrations for advertising, national magazines, and television networks. Prior to being an illustrator, she was an art director for several major publishing houses in New York. She has won awards for illustration, graphic design and for art direction from the NY Society of Illustrators, the Los Angeles Society of Illustrators, the New England Museum Association and from the Art Directors Club of New York. She lives in Maine.

What They're Saying About
Anthony Best:

★ "This story is rich in so many ways...a window into Asperger's syndrome and at the same time, a window into childhood.... I loved this story."
— Sima Gerber, *PhD professor of Speech/Language Pathology at Queens College*

★ "I think Anthony Best is a great avenue to teach typical children about their autistic friends and why they often act so differently."
— Kristen Mullaney, *parent of 2 children with autism*

★ "...the idea was fascinating, and the portrayal was clear and honest. This kind of a book can only do good things."
— Daniel Gottlieb, PhD, author of *Letters to Sam: A Grandfather's Lessons on Love, Loss and the Gifts of Life*